A Kid of Their Own

Megan Dowd Lambert
Illustrated by **Jessica Lanan**

ici **Charlesbridge**

For adoptees everywhere, and especially for my own kids, Natayja, Emilia, Stevie, and Caroline. Thank you for accepting me as your mom. I love you with all my heart.—M. D. L.

To families everywhere, no matter what they look like.—J. L.

Published by Charlesbridge, 85 Main Street,
Watertown, MA 02472
(617) 926-0329 • www.charlesbridge.com

At the time of publication, all URLs printed in this book were accurate and active. Charlesbridge, the author, and the illustrator are not responsible for the content or accessibility of any website.

Library of Congress Cataloging-in-Publication Data
Names: Lambert, Megan Dowd, author. | Lanan, Jessica, illustrator.
Title: A kid of their own / Megan Dowd Lambert; illustrated by Jessica Lanan.
Description: Watertown, MA: Charlesbridge, [2019] | Summary: Clyde has always taken his role of rooster at Sunrise Farm very seriously, but when Fran the goat and her hyperactive kid, Rowdy, join the other animals, Clyde's feathers are ruffled by all the attention that Rowdy is getting, and soon he is crowing at all hours just to wake up the kid—until all the animals tell him that they have had enough of his grandstanding.
Identifiers: LCCN 2017055932 | ISBN 9781580898799 (reinforced for library use) | ISBN 9781632897046 (ebook pdf) | ISBN 9781632897039 (e-book)
Subjects: LCSH: Roosters—Juvenile fiction. | Goats—Juvenile fiction. | Domestic animals—Juvenile fiction. | Jealousy—Juvenile fiction. | Adoption—Juvenile fiction. | CYAC: Roosters—Fiction. | Goats—Fiction. | Domestic animals—Fiction. | Jealousy—Fiction. | Adoption—Fiction.
Classification: LCC PZ7.1.L26 Ki 2019 | DDC [E]—dc23 LC record available at https://lccn.loc.gov/2017055932

Printed in China
(hc) 10 9 8 7 6 5 4 3 2 1

Illustrations done in watercolor on hot-press paper
Display type set in Fink Roman by Brand Design Co., Inc and Chaloops by Chank Co.
Text type set in ITC Goudy Sans by Bitstream Inc.
Color separations by Colourscan Print Co Pte Ltd, Singapore
Printed by 1010 Printing International Limited in Huizhou, Guangdong, China
Production supervision by Brian G. Walker
Designed by Susan Mallory Sherman and Diane M. Earley

Author's Note: *A Crow of His Own*, my first book set on Sunrise Farm, is about Clyde the rooster finding a distinctive voice, so rather than repeating the dialogue tags "said" or "asked," I played with a variety of verbs to describe and introduce speech. I do this again in *A Kid of Their Own* to underscore the idea that everyone's unique voice is important when creating an inclusive community.

OODLE-DOO!

A new day was dawning at Sunrise Farm, and Clyde was in the thick of it.

Clyde basked in the glow of everyone's
appreciation and settled in for a day of
resting his voice and a little light reading.
But suddenly he was interrupted.

"Meet Rowdy and Fran," Farmer Jay began.

"We can't ever have enough cheese," explained
Farmer Kevin. "And now we can make even more!"

As he watched the kid trip-trapping about,
Clyde wasn't so sure.

Roberta had always taken *him* under her wing.
But now she, more than anyone else, seemed charmed
by Rowdy horsing around the barnyard. With
jealous resolve, Clyde hatched a plan to recapture
her attention with an extra-special crow at dawn.

As the sun peeked over the hillside the next day, a determined Clyde assumed his position atop the coop, opened his beak, and . . .

"Don't what?" Clyde sputtered.

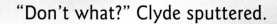

MAAAAAAAAAA!

"Oh dear!" exclaimed Roberta. "You woke up Rowdy, Clyde."

Clyde's feathers were ruffled. His wattle wobbled. "But I didn't even finish," he protested. "I always end with the 'doo' . . ."

"Well, maybe you should tone it down, for the kid's sake," Roberta fretted. And with that, she went to help Fran, leaving a dismayed Clyde in her wake.

Even though Clyde had a beak, his nose was out of joint. He did not tone it down. Instead, he crowed his crow not only at daybreak, but whenever Rowdy was resting in the barn.

"Oh my!" gasped Farmer Jay.

"Change is hard," said Farmer Kevin.

It's fair to say Clyde was getting Fran's goat with what she came to call his "maaaddening crow."

"I'm just doing my job," huffed a cocky Clyde when he saw everyone huddled around Rowdy.

But his righteousness quickly faded when he heard the others' comments.

Clyde was bereft. He brooded about the barnyard
until Roberta, who was nothing if not a motherly
goose, finally took him back under her wing.

"There, there, Clyde," she soothed. "It's hard
when the chickens come home to roost."

A sheepish Clyde swallowed his pride like so much chicken feed. "Would you help me talk with Fran?" he asked.

"Absolutely," agreed Roberta.

"Excuse me, Fran and Rowdy?" Clyde started.

"Yes?" Fran answered gruffly.

Ashamed of his foul behavior, Clyde was at a loss for words.

You can do it, Clyde.

But then a sleepy shake of Rowdy's floppy-eared head spurred the rooster into action.

Back at the coop, he rummaged through his special-occasions costume box.

The earmuffs were an impulse purchase that Clyde had regretted—until now.

You've got to be kidding.

"Now, they don't quite fit me," acknowledged Clyde, "but they're as good as new, and Rowdy can wear them to block out my morning crow." Fran ruminated on the idea. "I suppose we could give them a try," she conceded.

"No, they're not for eating, my sweet," corrected Fran.

And the next morning . . .

COCK-A-DOODL

Everyone *except* Rowdy stretched and entered the barnyard.

"Looks like my plan worked!" called Clyde.

"Yes," confirmed Fran. "He's fast asleep, thanks to those earmuffs of yours."

"They're his now. And I'm awfully sorry, Fran," Clyde apologized. "I was a perfect troll to you."

"Water under the bridge," accepted Fran. "And I'm sorry, too."

And that's how Clyde joined everyone in welcoming Fran and Rowdy, just in time for the farmers to bring home . . .